Text copyright © 1998 by Kate Banks. Pictures copyright © 1998 by Georg Hallensleben. Originally published in France by Gallimard Jeunesse.
All rights reserved. Distributed in Canada by Douglas & McIntyre Ltd. Printed and bound in Italy. First American edition, 1998

Library of Congress Cataloging-in-Publication Data
Banks, Kate, 1960–
      And if the moon could talk / Kate Banks ; pictures by Georg Hallensleben. — 1st American ed.
        p.   cm.
      "Frances Foster books"
      Summary: As evening progresses into nighttime, the moon looks down on a variety of nocturnal scenes, including a child getting ready for bed.
      ISBN 0-374-30299-5
      [1. Bedtime—Fiction. 2. Night—Fiction. 3. Moon—Fiction.] I. Hallensleben, Georg, ill. II. Title.
PZ7.B22594An   1998
[E]—dc21   97–29770

And If the Moon Could Talk

Kate Banks • Pictures by Georg Hallensleben

FRANCES FOSTER BOOKS

FARRAR STRAUS GIROUX   NEW YORK

Somewhere a pair of shoes lies under a chair.

A window yawns open. Twilight blazes a trail across the wall.

And if the moon could talk,
it would tell of evening
stealing through the woods
and a lizard scurrying home to supper.

Someone hums quietly. A clock ticks. A light flicks on.

And if the moon could talk,
it would tell of stars flaring up one by one
and a small fire burning by a tree.

Papa opens a book and turns the pages.

A story unfolds like a banner wandering across the sky.

And if the moon could talk,
it would tell of sand blowing across the desert
and nomads crouching by the dune.

On a small table sits a glass, a wooden boat, a starfish, too.

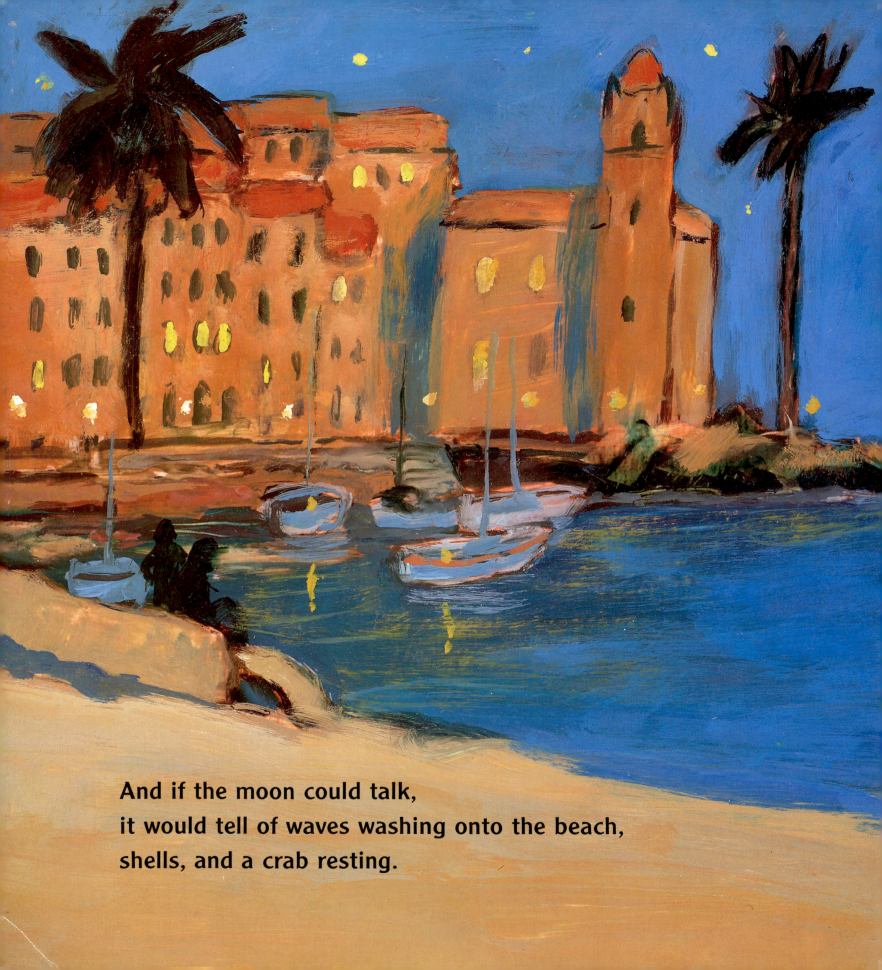

And if the moon could talk,
it would tell of waves washing onto the beach,
shells, and a crab resting.

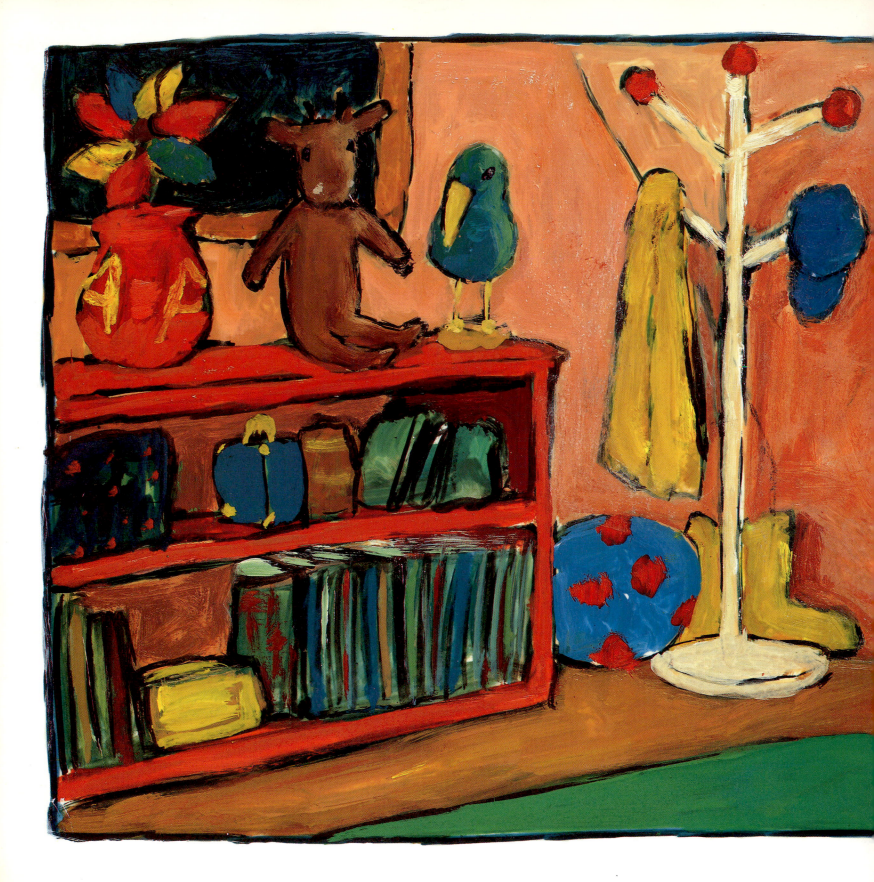

Music chimes from a small box on a shelf. A mobile stirs the air.

On a chair, a rabbit sits listening.

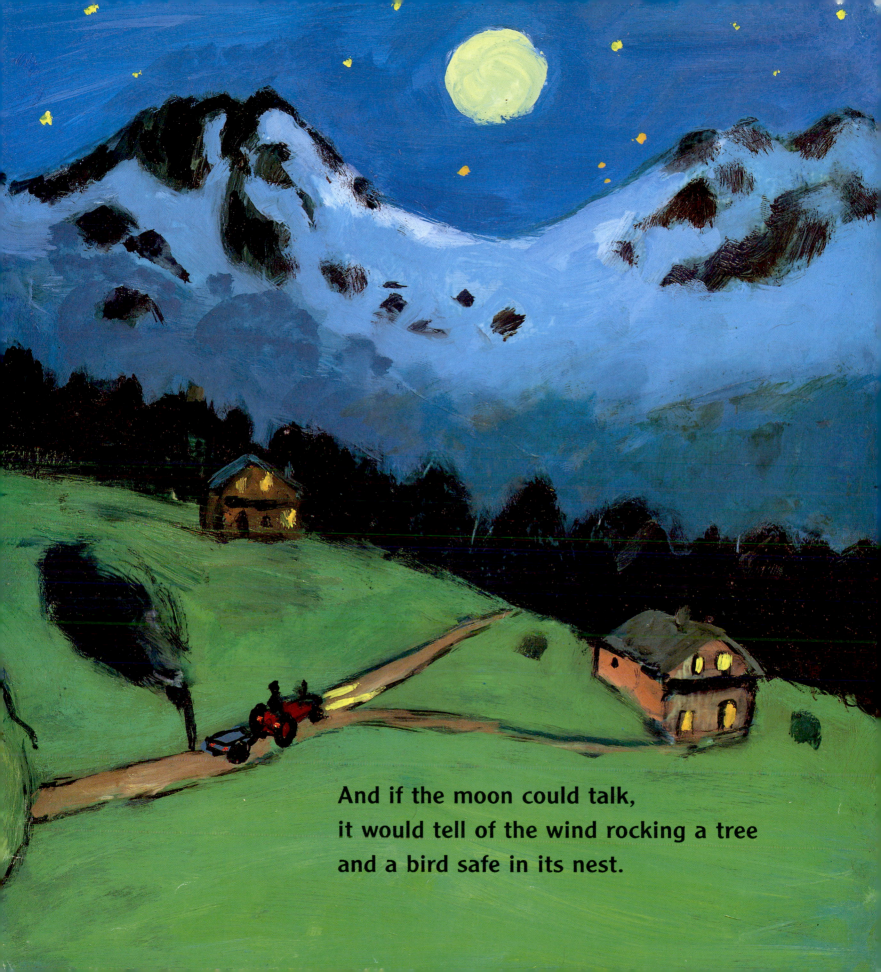

And if the moon could talk,
it would tell of the wind rocking a tree
and a bird safe in its nest.

Mama hands her child the rabbit.

She hugs her and pulls the blankets tight under her chin.

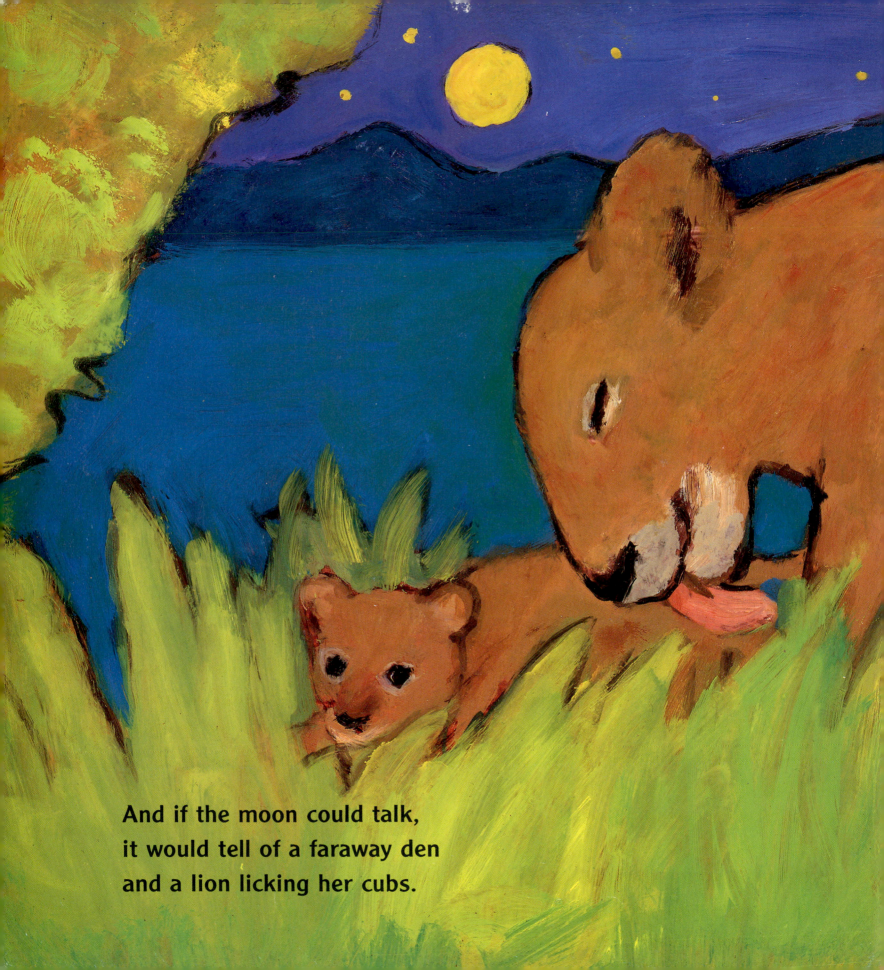

And if the moon could talk,
it would tell of a faraway den
and a lion licking her cubs.

Eyes close. There is a drowsy hush.

Darkness swells into a colorful dream.

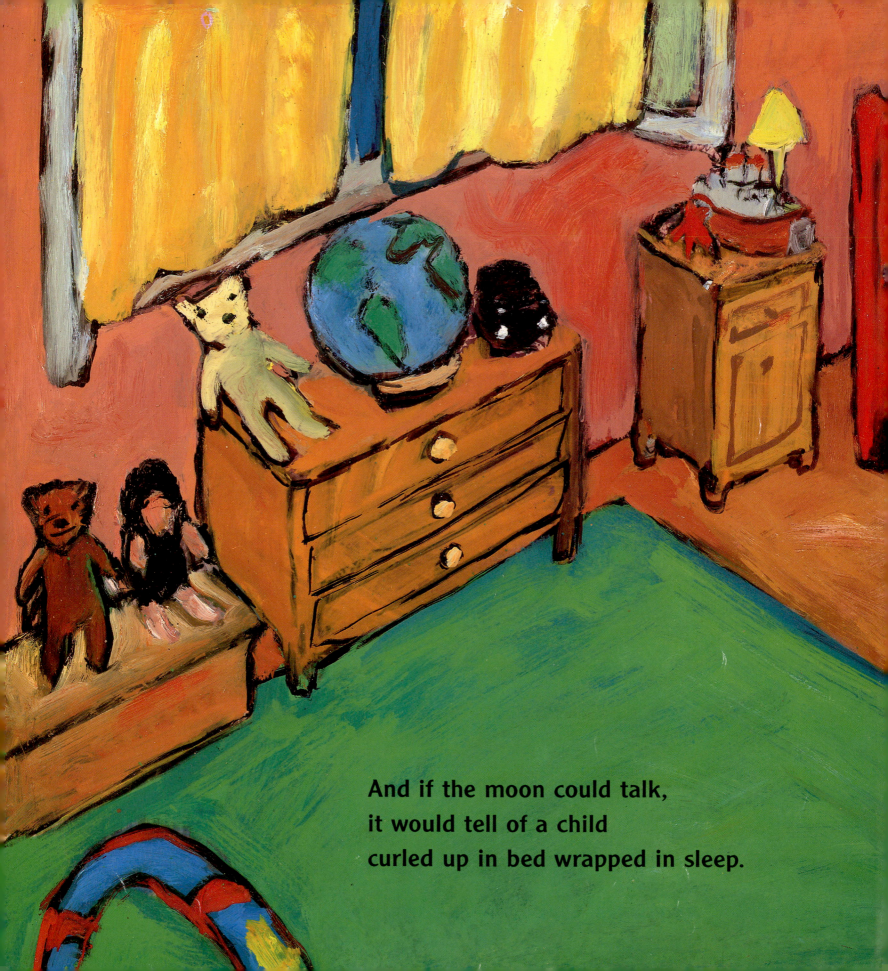

And if the moon could talk,
it would tell of a child
curled up in bed wrapped in sleep.

And it would murmur

Good night.